MW01639973

MY FIRST LOOK
AT VEHICLES

Airplanes soar high above the ground

Airplanes

Cathy Tatge

Creative Education

Published by Creative Education

P.O. Box 227, Mankato, Minnesota 56002

Creative Education is an imprint of The Creative Company

Designed by Rita Marshall

Photographs by Artemis Images (ATD Group, Inc.), Corbis (Hulton-Deutsch Archive, George Hall, Underwood & Underwood), Defense Visual Information Center, Gregory Fischer, Getty Images (AFP, The Image Bank, Photographer's Choice, Taxi), Richard Gross, Derk R. Kuyper, Sally McCrae Kuyper, North Wind Picture Archives, Otto G. Richter Library (Archives & Special Collections, University of Miami, Coral Gables, Florida), Bonnie Sue Rauch, Reuters (Doug Wilson), D. Jeanene Tiner, John Wilson

Printed in the United States of America

Library of Congress Cataloging-in-Publication Data

Tatge, Cathy. Airplanes / by Cathy Tatge.

p. cm. – (My first look at vehicles)

Includes index.

ISBN-13: 978-1-58341-525-2

1. Airplanes—Juvenile literature. I. Title. II. Series.

TL547.b.T326 2007 629.133'34—dc22 2006027445

First edition 9 8 7 6 5 4 3 2 1

Airplanes

In the Sky

Airplanes are vehicles that fly through the sky. They do not go on roads like cars do. They travel above cities and roads. They can go over deep oceans. They can go over high mountains. They can even go above the clouds!

Before people had airplanes, they made gliders. Gliders looked like wings that were strapped on to a person. To glide, people

Airplanes can fly over fluffy clouds

had to run fast up a hill. Then they jumped off the top! They flew through the air. But gliders were dangerous and hard to steer. They only worked from the top of a hill.

Airplanes Long Ago

Orville and Wilbur Wright (*RITE*) were brothers. They loved to fly and used gliders. But the Wright brothers wanted to **invent** a glider that was easier to control. They wanted to go farther. They also wanted to make flying safer.

Before the Wright
brothers made the airplane,
they made bicycles.

THE FIRST GLIDERS WERE NOT EASY TO USE

The Wrights watched birds to see how they flew. They learned that a glider needed strong wings. They also needed something to make the glider move on its own.

In 1903, the Wrights made a glider with an **engine**. They called it the *Flyer*. It was the first airplane to fly. But it stayed in the air for only 12 seconds!

Charles Lindbergh was the first **pilot** to fly alone across the Atlantic Ocean.

THE *FLYER* FLEW LOW OVER THE GROUND

Planes That Work

Today, airplanes do many jobs. Planes can go much faster than cars, trains, or boats. They can go many places other vehicles cannot go.

Crop dusters are planes that help farmers. They spray things on the fields to make the plants grow. They also help get rid of bugs.

Some planes have two sets of wings, one on top of the other. They are called biplanes.

SOME BIPLANES ARE USED AS CROP DUSTERS

Some planes can land on water. These are called seaplanes. Seaplanes have **pontoons** on the bottom instead of wheels. They take food and other things to small islands.

Other planes carry only people. These are called passenger planes. The Concorde was one of the fastest passenger planes. It flew 1,350 miles (2,173 km) per hour!

Seaplanes need calm water to land on

At an Airport

To ride on a plane, people go to an airport. Airports have long, flat roads called runways. This is where the planes land and take off.

When planes are not on the runway, they are stored in hangars. A hangar is like a garage for airplanes. People check the planes to make sure that everything works.

Jets like the Concorde fly very fast. They are faster than the speed of sound!

The Concorde flew far above other airplanes

UNITED EXPRESS

Airplanes take off and land day and night

In bad weather, planes have to stay on the ground. It is dangerous to fly in storms. But when the weather is good, it is fun to ride in planes!

PILOTS HAVE TO BE EXTRA CAREFUL WHEN IT RAINS

Hands-on: Paper Planes

You can make your own airplane out of paper!

What You Need

A piece of paper

What You Do

1. Fold the paper in half lengthwise to make a crease. Open the piece of paper.
2. Fold the two top corners toward the center.
3. Fold each side toward the center again.
4. Fold each side toward the center one more time.
5. Bend the last fold back. This is the bottom of your airplane. Can you make it fly?

THERE ARE ALWAYS LOTS OF AIRPLANES IN THE SKY

Index

Words to Know

engine—a machine that makes an airplane move

invent—to make something that no one else has ever made

pilot—a person who flies a plane

pontoons—boat-shaped tubes that help planes land on water

Read More

Bingham, Caroline, ed. *Big Book of Airplanes*. New York: DK Publishing, 2001.

Munsch, Robert N. *Angela's Airplane*. Toronto: Annick Press, 1988.

Shea, George. *First Flight: The Story of Tom Tate and the Wright Brothers*. New York: HarperCollins, 1997.

Explore the Web

Aviation and Space Education Outreach Program: Kids Corner
http://www.faa.gov/education—research/education/student_resources/kids_corner/ages_5_9/

How Things Fly http://www.nasm.si.edu/exhibitions/gal109/gal109.html

Phoenix Sky Harbor Kids' Corner http://phoenix.gov/AVIATION/kids/index.html